THIS WALKER BOOK BELONGS TO:

_____

_____

THE LITTLE RIDERS

The Little Riders is set in Nazi-occupied Holland during the Second World War. A timeless story of courage, forgiveness and true friendship, it is as fresh and relevant today as it was when first published many years ago.

The author, Margaretha Shemin, was born in Alkmaar, a mediaeval town about twenty miles north of Amsterdam. In the centre of the town is a tower where, to this day, little riders come out as the clock strikes – just as they do in this story.

Peter Spier, the illustrator, was also born in Holland, but now lives in the USA, the home of Johanna, the heroine of *The Little Riders*. He is a former winner of the Caldecott Medal – America's most important prize for book illustration.

The
LITTLE
RIDERS

by Margaretha Shemin
illustrated by Peter Spier

WALKER BOOKS
LONDON

To Dédé

First published 1963 in the USA by
Coward, McCann & Geoghegan Inc.
Reissued in the USA 1988 by
G.P. Putnam's Sons
First published in Great Britain 1988 by
Julia MacRae Books
This edition published 1990 by
Walker Books Ltd, 87 Vauxhall Walk
London SE11 5HJ

Text © 1963, 1988 Margaretha Shemin
Illustrations © 1963, 1988 Peter Spier

Printed in Great Britain by
Richard Clay Ltd, Bungay, Suffolk

British Library Cataloguing in Publication Data
Shemin, Margaretha
The little riders.
I. Title II. Spier, Peter
813'.514 [J]
ISBN 0-7445-1751-6

Chapter One

Johanna was sitting on the windowsill, in her little attic room, waiting for the clock on the church steeple to strike twelve. It was a very warm summer day and her window was opened wide. From her window, Johanna had the best view of the church steeple in the whole town. That was why it was her favourite spot.

Once when her father was a little boy, he had slept in that same room and had sat on the windowsill waiting for the clock to strike twelve. He had waited for the doors under the church steeple to open, just as Johanna was doing now. And he had counted the twelve little riders as they rode out on their white horses. Johanna always thought of her father at this time of the day, as she sat on the windowsill.

It had been a long time since she had been home in America with her parents. She couldn't even remember her father very clearly. He was a sea captain, and because he had become very lonesome on his long voyages, he had decided to take Johanna's mother with him on one of them. So he had sent Johanna to Holland to visit her grandparents.

She remembered as clearly as if it happened yesterday how she had said good-bye to her father and mother. She had kissed them both and tried very hard to show them a happy face.

While her father had held her in his arms, he had said to her, "Thank you very much, my little Johanna, for giving me Mother for such a long time. Think of me when you are in my country and don't forget to give my very special love to the little riders in the church steeple. Help Grandfather take care of them, so that when I come with Mother to bring you back home, they will ride for us, whenever the church clock strikes."

Now Johanna had been in Holland more than four years. Soon after she had come to her grandparents the war in Europe had broken out, and less than a year later, in the early days of May, Holland had been invaded by the German army. For the people of Holland, who had always loved their freedom more than anything else in the world, the presence of the German soldiers was very hard to bear.

From her window seat Johanna looked down over the town. It was an old town with a canal around the centre. Behind the canal were the strong fortifications that had once protected the town from enemies that threatened from outside. Her grandparents' house stood at the marketplace, where all the old houses were huddled together, as if they were leaning on each other for support. There were few people in the streets, mostly women and children. It was dangerous these days for men to be out in the streets, since at any time they could be seized and taken far away to work for the Germans.

Johanna looked again at the hands of the big clock on the church steeple. Soon it would be twelve o'clock. After the clock had struck twelve times, the little doors under the steeple would open up and out would come the little riders.

Grandfather had told Johanna all he knew about the history of the little riders. They were as old as the town, and that was many hundreds of years. They were figures of twelve young noblemen who had gone out as crusaders to the Holy Land and who had never returned to the town. Long ago an artisan had made the figures out of lead and ever since they had ridden over the town, sitting proud and erect on their horses.

When the air was still trembling with the last stroke of the clock, six little riders would come out of each door. They would ride up to each other, lift their swords in a salute and then go in the opposite door. In and out as many times as the clock had struck. While they rode in and out of the doors, the carillon of the church played old Dutch folk tunes. The music was carried all over town and could be heard in even the farthest street and in every house where the windows were open.

Ever since Johanna's grandfather was a young man, he had taken care of the church, and his most important task was to take care of the little riders. He was the only man in the town who understood the complex mechanism that made the little riders ride out over the town, every hour, day and night. Johanna helped her grandfather take care of the riders, just as her father had done when he was a small boy, and Johanna loved the little riders just as much as her father did. She always looked up at them, wherever she was in town, when the hour struck. But she always tried to be in her room, where she could see them best, when the clock struck twelve, because then, of course, they rode the longest. Now the clock was already striking the hour and the few women and children down in the quiet marketplace looked up at the church steeple to see the little riders. But just when the clock had struck for the twelfth time and the little doors opened up to let out the first riders, and when the carillon started to play its music, the gay melodies were drowned out.

Towards the marketplace came the sound of oncoming marching. It sounded to Johanna like the rolling of heavy thunder. Those hundreds and hundreds of soldiers' boots – they sounded as if they would trample away the cobblestones of the old marketplace. At the same time all the soldiers started to sing. Nothing could be heard any more of the brave little tunes the carillon sent high up into the sky. But the riders kept riding proud and erect on their little horses.

11

Johanna averted her eyes from the marketplace to avoid seeing the soldiers. She closed the window so that she wouldn't hear how loud their voices were. But the window didn't keep out the noise. While she watched the riders make their salutes and ride busily in and out the little doors, she could still hear the marching and the singing and the shouting and she became afraid. She remembered again what she had almost forgotten during her busy morning – how different Grandfather had looked to her that morning and how long it had taken him to walk up the steps to the church steeple. How worried he had seemed as he looked at the riders who were waiting so patiently behind the little doors to ride out.

Now the last rider had disappeared and Johanna slipped from her windowsill. Dinner was at twelve o'clock and even now, when there wasn't much to eat, Grandmother did not allow anybody to be late. She quickly walked down the stairs. There was nobody in the hall but the door to the small vestibule was closed and she could hear voices behind it.

When Johanna entered the living room where they, like most Dutch families, always had their meals, she saw to her surprise that the table hadn't even been set. She went back into the hall to find Grandfather and Grandmother. But she stopped when she saw them. They were standing at the foot of the stairs and with them was a German soldier. They spoke in low voices and Johanna couldn't hear what they were saying. They went upstairs and all she could hear now was the sound of their footsteps and the opening and closing of doors. The stairs to the attic creaked as they went up to her room.

It seemed a long time before they came down again. Grandfather's and Grandmother's voices didn't sound low now. They were loud and angry. The German soldier was walking ahead of them. Then Johanna didn't look any more and she turned her head away. At the beginning of the war, she had made herself a promise never to look a German soldier in the face because she couldn't bear the sight of them.

Chapter Two

Dinner that day was especially good. Grandfather had gone fishing that morning and had caught a big bass. There were boiled potatoes with the fish and Grandmother had picked the first red, ripe strawberries from her garden. But nobody ate much. Everybody was quiet. There was only the tinkling of the knives and forks against the plates. A housefly buzzed against the window screen, trying to fly out into the sun. Outside there was no sound to be heard. Everybody ate at this hour of the day and the marketplace was lying lost and forgotten in the hot sunshine.

Grandfather put down his knife and fork and pushed his only half-empty plate away. He looked

straight at Johanna and his eyes were filled with pride and love.

"There is bad news today, Johanna," he said, "but nothing so bad that we can't bear it. The German soldier you heard talking to us before dinner came to requisition a room in our house for a German officer, a certain Captain Braun. I explained to him that we used all the rooms and didn't have one room to spare. He never listened to me."

Grandfather got up from his chair and walked over to the window. He opened the screen a little to let out the fly that had kept buzzing desperately.

"He took your room," Grandfather continued, and sat down again. "There was nothing I could do about it, although I tried very hard for you."

Johanna had to swallow a few times before she could speak. "When will he come?" she asked.

"Late in the afternoon." It was Grandmother who answered. "We'd better finish dinner now. We'll need all afternoon, Johanna, to move your things out of your room. You will sleep on the couch upstairs in Grandfather's den."

Grandmother took the dishes to the kitchen and Johanna followed her. She was still too stunned to speak. It had all happened so unexpectedly. It would be dreadful to have somebody she really hated in her own house, in her own room. And Johanna hated the German soldiers. She hated the sound of their boots as they marched, always singing, through the narrow streets of the town. She hated their laughing and their loud shouts of "Heil Hitler". She hated the soldiers when they posted the big white bulletins on the corners of the streets, telling of new hostages they had taken and of many hateful orders given by the German town commander. Most of all she hated them because they wouldn't let her go back to her father and mother in America.

It would also be extremely dangerous, Johanna realised, to have one of them in the house. Johanna knew about the radio hidden in Grandfather's den and the weekly meetings Grandfather held upstairs. She knew there were many other dangerous secrets that Grandfather and Grandmother had never told her. All these secrets the house had kept within its walls, and the house had been the only safe place in a world full of enemies and danger. Now the house had been invaded too.

All afternoon Johanna helped Grandmother. She took all her clothes out of the attic cupboard. Now that the cupboard was empty she could almost see the cubbyhole hiding all the way at the back of the cupboard. It had always been Johanna's secret hiding place. She opened the small door that was only big enough for her to crawl through. In the cubbyhole were some of her old toys, her teddy bear that had travelled with her all the way from America to Holland and some seashells her father had once brought back for her from a far country. She never played with them any more, but she didn't want to leave them with Captain Braun. She couldn't take the cubbyhole with her, Johanna thought angrily. She hoped that Captain Braun would never discover it. Last of all she took her books and the pictures of her father and mother and the white house with the shutters, where she had lived in America. Now the room was empty.

Downstairs, Johanna tried to make Grandfather's den look a little like her own room, but it was a small dark room and Johanna had never liked it. It smelled old and musty. She didn't even want to put the bright, gay pictures on the wall, although Grandfather had made room for them. Her attic room was bright and sunny, but here was only one small window, through which the sun never shone. The den looked out on the narrow side street off the marketplace, and right across the street rose the high grey wall of the church. She could see only a small piece of sky, if she leaned far enough out of the window. And no matter how far she leaned out, she could never see the little riders up under the belfry.

Late in the afternoon Captain Braun arrived. He rang the bell softly. Grandfather went to open the door for him as Grandmother and Johanna stood in the hall. Johanna thought, Now he will enter our house and he will stick out his hand and shout "Heil Hitler", and what will Grandfather do when he hears those words spoken in his house?

But Captain Braun only clicked his heels and made a little bow in the direction of Grandmother. She gave him a stiff nod. He stretched out his hand to Grandfather. He and Grandfather were both tall men and could look each other straight in the face without looking up or down. Grandfather looked at Captain Braun and gave him the same stiff nod that Grandmother had given him. He did not take the hand that was stretched out to him.

Captain Braun was looking down at Johanna, but she saw only his big heavy polished boots and the horrible grey colour of his uniform. When he tried to speak a few friendly words to her in broken Dutch, she thought more than ever of the promise she had made herself, never to look a German soldier in the face. She turned her head away from him. For a moment it seemed that Captain Braun didn't know what to do or say. He clicked his heels again and made another stiff bow in the direction of Grandfather and Grandmother.

"I apologise to you," he said in broken Dutch. "I will try to cause no trouble to you. I wish you all a good evening." Then he turned directly to Grandfather. "Would you be kind, sir, and show me the room?"

Grandfather didn't speak but led Captain Braun to the stairs and mounted them quickly. Captain Braun picked up his heavy sack and followed slowly. Johanna could hear the sack bump heavily on every step till it was carried all the way high up to her attic room. Then she heard the door close and Grandfather's footsteps coming downstairs.

Johanna went to bed early that night. She had felt tired, but now she couldn't fall asleep. She kept tossing in her new bed. There were strange, unfamiliar shadows on the wall. The big grey wall of the church seemed so near, ready to fall on top of the room. Faintly, she heard the clock strike ten times. Then the door was opened very softly and Grandfather came into the room. He sat down in the chair next to Johanna's bed and took her hand in his own.

"Why don't you sleep, Johanna?" he asked. "You should try to sleep now. We have all had a hard day and so much has happened."

"I hate him," Johanna said, "and I hate this room, too. From here I can see only the grey wall of the church. I can't see the riders, I can't even hear the carillon very clearly. How can I ever fall asleep without the little riders? I always watched

them just before I went to sleep. In the morning the carillon woke me up. Now he has my room that once was Father's room. He has no right to be there. He has no right to sit there and watch the riders and listen to the carillon."

Grandfather got up from the chair and walked over to the window. He looked up at the grey wall of the church.

"Captain Braun," he said, "will never see the little riders ride out on their horses and he will never hear the carillon. Today an ordinance came from the town commander. The riders are not allowed to ride any more and the carillon may not play any more. I just went to the church tower."

Grandfather turned away from the window and paced up and down the small room.

"All these years I have taken care of the riders, so that they could ride when the clock struck the hour. But tonight I closed the little doors."

Johanna sat up in her bed, her arms around her thin knees. Her face looked small and white, her eyes big and dark.

"Why?" she asked Grandfather. "Why may the little riders not ride out any more?"

"They didn't give us any reasons," Grandfather answered, "but we have seen this coming for a long time. This ordinance is only the beginning. The little riders are made of lead. The Germans need metal and they may throw them into a melting pot to make munitions out of them for their armies. Everywhere the occupied countries are being plundered, their treasures taken away and the bells of their churches melted down to be made into weapons. Grandmother and I have often talked of what to do if this ever threatened to happen to the little riders."

Grandfather patted Johanna's hand gently. "We will have to hide the riders, Johanna, if we want to keep them for the town. Go to sleep now, there is much to be done tomorrow."

Grandfather tucked the blanket around Johanna and left the room, but Johanna didn't want to sleep. She wanted to think about everything Grandfather had told her. The night was cool and quiet. From somewhere she heard the sound of a flute. At first she thought it must come from outside. She pushed her blanket away and stepped out of her bed to look out of the small window. But she saw only the dark street and the high grey wall of the church across it and she didn't hear a sound. She walked across the room and opened the door to the hall. The sound came from the top of the house. Barefoot, Johanna climbed silently up the attic stairs. Halfway up she could see her room.

Captain Braun had left the door open so that the cool night wind could blow through the warm room. He was sitting on Johanna's windowsill. His back was turned to the door, his long legs dangling out of the window. And he played his flute over the silent marketplace.

Johanna didn't watch him for long. She went downstairs without making a noise. She didn't close her door with a bang, but she closed it very firmly. When she was back in bed, she pulled the cover over her ears so that she couldn't hear a sound that could keep her awake. But it was a long time before she fell asleep.

Chapter Three

The next day, everybody looked up at the church steeple, wondering what had happened. It was the first time in many hundreds of years that the little riders had not ridden out and the carillon had not played. Soon the town buzzed with the news of the ordinance from the town commander.

After a few days something happened – something of such tremendous importance that the Germans had suddenly much more urgent and grave matters on their minds than the twelve little riders high up on the church tower. Even Grandfather didn't think any more about hiding them.

Johanna was sitting with Grandfather and Grandmother in the den, listening to the radio hidden behind the books in the bookcase. Then the big news came crackling and almost inaudible, and none of them dared to believe it was true. Allied armies had landed in France. All morning long, Johanna and her grandparents kept the radio on. They had to hear over and over again the crackling voice that kept repeating the same bulletin.

In the afternoon Grandfather turned off the radio and they went for a walk. It was a clear, cool summer day. People stood together in their front yards, discussing the news in low voices. There were no marching or singing soldiers in the streets of the town today. The few single soldiers who passed by seemed to be in a hurry and did not pay attention to anyone. For one brief moment the town seemed to belong again to its people.

Johanna thought of her mother and father. She had never doubted that her father would come with the liberators. Now maybe he would come soon. He would help free Holland and take her back home with him. At night lying in bed, she had imagined many different ways that he might come to her. Sometimes she imagined that he would be an officer in the American navy and he would come on a big battleship. Sometimes she thought of him as a pilot flying a big aeroplane. But now she hoped that he would be with the first troops that had just landed in France. She always imagined how he would stretch out his arms to her and lift her high up in the air, as he always had done when he came home from his long trips. He would say, "My little Johanna," and she would look into his blue eyes. But then Johanna always had to stop imagining because she couldn't think about the rest of his face.

Grandfather and Grandmother and Johanna spent much time upstairs in the den, listening to the radio. At first the liberating armies advanced fast. The south of Holland was free. Then the days became weeks and the weeks became months. The liberation of the north still seemed sure, but not so near any more. Johanna still dreamed about her father, but she was afraid he would not come soon.

Life went on as it had in the four years before. Grandfather started to think again about a safe hiding place for the little riders because now, more than ever, the Germans needed every scrap of metal for ammunition.

Every evening Grandfather went up to the

church steeple. The last light of the long summer days came through the oval window. He worked with endless patience to take apart the mechanism that for so many years had made the riders ride out on their horses while the carillon played the old folk tunes.

Now Johanna was almost used to the presence of Captain Braun in the house, but still she had never seen his face. In the morning she met him on the stairs, she going down for breakfast, he going up to his room after morning drill. In the evening she met him again, she going up to the den, he going down on his way out for dinner. He always said "Good morning" and "Good evening". Johanna always turned her head away from him and never answered. He walked softly in his heavy boots except when he had to ask Grandfather or Grandmother something. Then he stamped noisily with his boots so that they could hear him long before he knocked on the door. There was always time to hide the radio behind the books in the bookcase.

At night now Johanna sometimes forgot to close the door of her room and she could hear the music of the flute. When the summer nights were quiet, Captain Braun always played. But often now the air outside was filled with the droning sound of heavy aeroplanes flying over. On such nights Johanna climbed out of her bed and leaned far out the window to see their lights high against the dark sky. She knew that many of them were American planes and she imagined that her father might be in one of them. They were aeroplanes flying over to drop their bombs on the towns of Germany. On those nights Captain Braun did not play his flute.

One day when Captain Braun had gone out, Johanna went upstairs and looked at her old room. Her cupboard was full of coats and army caps with the German eagle on them. Pairs of heavy shiny boots stood in a neat row on her shoe shelf. Johanna had to push aside the heavy uniforms to get to the back of the cupboard. She wanted to have a look at her secret hiding place. The bolt on the small door seemed untouched and dusty. When she opened it and crawled through the door, the cubbyhole was empty, as she had left it. Captain Braun had probably never discovered it. She had to touch the uniforms again to make them hang as they had before she had pushed them aside. She closed the door quickly and wiped her hands on her skirt.

On the wall, where once her pictures had hung, were now pictures of Captain Braun's family. In one, an older lady and an older man were standing arm in arm in a garden full of flowers. In another, a young woman and a laughing boy were standing on skis in dazzling white snow. It was strange to see real Germans in a garden full of flowers and with skis on a sunny mountain slope. On the table with some music books was the flute in a black velvet case embroidered with mountain flowers, blue gentians and silver-white edelweiss. Johanna wondered who had made the little case. The old lady from the flower garden or the young woman on skis? She decided that the old lady would probably be better at embroidering.

Before Johanna left the room she sat down on her windowsill and looked at the church steeple. The little doors were closed now and the steeple looked old and grey, like any other church steeple.

"Don't worry, little riders," Johanna whispered to the closed doors. "It will be all right, the Germans will not get you." Tonight, Grandfather had told her, there would be a meeting in the den about the little riders.

"We cannot hide the riders without asking the townspeople, Johanna," Grandfather had said.

"There is too much at stake. If the Germans find the riders gone, they may punish the whole town. This isn't something we may do on our own." But Johanna was sure that the people of the town would never let the little riders fall into the hands of the German soldiers.

It was a good night to have the meeting, for it was Friday, the night Captain Braun was usually not home. It was a black night outside and raining heavily. Several months ago the town commander had imposed a curfew on the town and no civilians, except a few who had passes, were allowed to be out in the streets from eight o'clock in the evening until six o'clock the next morning.

One by one Grandfather's friends came to the house. They came huddled inside their raincoats, hugging close to the grey walls of the church. The rain and the darkness made them almost invisible. Each one pressed the doorbell six short times and Johanna opened the door just wide enough for one person to creep in. Then she closed the door again. When they had all arrived and gone upstairs, Johanna put on her raincoat and went outside. She left the front door open a little. She sat down behind the lilac bush next to the front door, where she could overlook the whole market-place, but could still get back into the house unseen, if she saw something suspicious and needed to warn Grandfather. Grandmother sat at the side entrance of the house, watching the street.

Johanna became cold and wet, sitting behind the lilac bush. The rain fell heavier and dripped from the roof in a little stream down her neck. The night was windy too, and now and then she had to close her eyes when the wet branches of the bush swept against her face. Her legs were stiff and cramped, but she didn't dare to change her position much.

What took the men so long? She had been sure that they would decide to hide the riders, but now she started to doubt. Could there be some among them who didn't think the riders worth the risk of hiding? If she could only go up for a minute and hear what was being said. But she could not leave her post.

And now she heard footsteps coming from the other side of the marketplace and then drawing near. Someone was whistling. It could only be a German, Johanna thought bitterly. No one else could walk so free in the night through the streets of their town, whistling a little tune in the rain. The steps came nearer and nearer and the tune began to sound familiar. It was Captain Braun coming back earlier than usual. Quickly Johanna went into the house and closed the door behind her. She ran upstairs and knocked on the door of Grandfather's den. Immediately the talking inside stopped and the lights went out. Johanna went all the way to the back of the dark hall and waited. She saw Captain Braun come up the stairs. He had left the lights off and walked softly with his boots in his hands as if he didn't want to wake the sleeping house.

One by one, as they had come, the men left the house. It was still raining and the darkness would protect them until they reached their homes. Johanna was alone now with Grandfather. She didn't dare to ask him what had been decided. Grandmother came in carrying three cups of hot imitation tea and slices of plain bread on a tray. The three of them sat around the table.

"They didn't even give me a chance to deliver the long speech I prepared in advance," Grandfather said. "There was never any doubt in anybody's mind what to do. The Germans will never have the little riders. After the war is over and we are liberated, they will ride again over our town."

Suddenly Johanna felt hungry, and she took a big bite from her slice of bread.

"I never doubted that we would decide to hide the little riders," Grandfather continued. "I worked on it all these long summer evenings. Everything is ready now. It will take only a few minutes to bring them down." Grandfather got up from his chair to look out of the window into the dark and rainy night. "There is no moon tonight and it's still raining heavily. There won't be a single German in the streets. We may never have a chance like this again. We'll hide the riders tonight, but we must wait till it's a little later."

"We'll wake you, Johanna," Grandmother said. "Try now first to get some sleep." She left the room with Grandfather.

Johanna didn't undress. She opened the door a little and lay down on top of her bed. The night was loud with the sounds of the wind and the rain, but there were no aeroplanes overhead. For the first time in many nights Captain Braun played his flute again. The melody was a lazy, drowsy one. It made Johanna feel warm and happy inside and it made her very sleepy.

Johanna must have slept a few hours before Grandfather came to her bed and tugged her arm gently. She got up quickly. Downstairs, Grandmother was already dressed in her coat with a dark scarf tied around her head. They left the house by the side door. The door of the church tower was opposite, but there was the narrow street between that led to the marketplace. Grandfather crossed the street first to open the door. Then came Grandmother and last, Johanna.

Inside the tower it was completely dark. Grandfather had climbed the steps so often that he led the way. No one talked and Johanna could not remember that the steps had ever seemed so long and steep. As they climbed higher, the sound of the wind and rain came louder and louder. Grandfather had already reached the top of the stairs and now he handed the riders and the horses to Grandmother and Johanna.

The staircase was so narrow and steep they could take only one rider at a time. It was too dark for Johanna to see the little rider that she carried. She could only feel the cool metal against her hands. The rider was bigger than she had expected, reaching up almost to her waist when for a moment she put him next to her on one of the steps. She could feel the hands that held the sword, smaller than her own trembling hands. She started to carry him down. The rider, although made of lead, was hollow inside and not too heavy, but was clumsy to carry on the narrow, steep staircase. Each trip across the street and back up the church tower was harder than the one before. The last little rider seemed heaviest of all. Grandfather made one more trip to lock the door of the church tower.

In their own house they had to be careful to make no noise that could waken Captain Braun, but here the stairs were wider and Grandfather and Grandmother could carry two riders at a time. Johanna felt weak and shaky when the last rider with his horse was finally carried safely into Grandfather's den.

Grandfather locked the door and closed the curtains at the window. He turned on the light. Johanna kneeled down and looked into the proud and brave faces of the little riders.

Chapter Four

For that one night the riders were hidden in Grandfather's den under the couch that was now Johanna's bed. The next morning Grandfather would try to find a place where they could stay hidden until the war was over, some place far away where no German would think of looking.

Johanna went to bed exhausted but happier than she had been in many weeks. The little riders would be safe. If she reached under her bed, she could feel the curly mane of one of the horses. Outside, the night cleared, the rain stopped and the wind died down. A few stars appeared and with them, like more stars, came the lights of aeroplanes overhead. Their buzzing sound gave Johanna a safe feeling and made her drowsy. Just before she fell asleep she thought again of her father. He walked towards her, taking long, impatient steps. He lifted her high in the air and said, "Give my very special love to the little riders and help Grandfather take care of them."

The next morning after breakfast Grandfather went to a nearby village where he had a friend who was a farmer. Dirk was one of the few farmers who had been allowed to keep his horse and wagon. Because he delivered eggs and fresh milk several times a week to the house of the German town commander, the German sentries who stood guard at the entrances of the town never searched his wagon. Many times young men who were hiding from the Germans had left town in Dirk's wagon, hidden underneath the tarpaulin between the empty egg boxes and the rattling milk containers. Grandfather and Dirk had often worked together to take such young men to safer places in the country and Grandfather was sure Dirk would help hide the little riders.

Grandfather was gone most of the day. He came back around tea-time. Grandmother and

Johanna had just started to worry about what might have delayed him, when Grandfather entered the house. He was happy and pleased. Everything was going to work out beautifully. Dirk had given him twenty-four heavy burlap sacks. In the course of the evening Grandfather's friends would come, unseen through the dark, and each would take home a sack with a rider or horse in it. The next morning they would take the sacks to the small café near the edge of town where Dirk always stopped on his way home for a cup of coffee and a game of billiards with his friends. In the small room behind the bar many people had waited to be taken to safety by Dirk's horse and wagon. The little riders and their horses would wait there now. And they would stay hidden on Dirk's farm until they could return to the church steeple.

It was still a few hours before dark. Grandfather and Johanna went upstairs to put the riders and their horses in the burlap sacks so that they could be taken away without delay when the men came. Johanna looked for the last time at the riders' faces. With her hands she covered their small hands that so many times had lifted the swords in proud salutes to each other. The Germans will not get them, she thought. They will always ride over the town. Even a hundred years from now.

It was still light when Johanna and Grandfather finished and went downstairs. Grandmother picked up her knitting at the round table in the living room. Grandfather sucked on an empty pipe and Johanna leafed through an old magazine. The curfew would start soon and, except for the bark of a dog and the cooing of the doves that nested under the eaves of the church tower, it was quiet outside.

Then, from the side street that led to the marketplace, came the sound of marching soldiers. It was unusual for a group of soldiers to be exercising at this late hour. Now that they came nearer, they sounded not so much like a group of soldiers exercising, but more like eight or ten soldiers who, by force of habit, marched instead of walking. They came out of the side street into the marketplace.

"God knows what they are up to," Grandmother said, "but it's never good if they come by night."

"And there are quite a number of them." Grandfather looked out of the window. "They never use so many for a simple arrest."

"But they do if they search..." A house,

Johanna was going to say, but she didn't complete her sentence.

One of the soldiers shouted a command and the group stopped still. They were in front of the house. Grandfather quickly stepped back from the window into the dark room.

"They may have come for something else." He tried to reassure Grandmother and Johanna.

The doorbell rang loudly and insistently and Grandfather went to open the door. Grandmother and Johanna followed him into the hall. Nine soldiers were standing on the doorstep and one of them was the spokesman. Johanna was so frightened that for the first time since the beginning of the war, she forgot all about her promise and looked the soldier straight in the face. She saw a large man with a big, red face and two small shiny eyes under shaggy eyebrows. He spoke to Grandfather in heavily accented but otherwise good Dutch that Johanna could easily understand.

"We are sent by the town commander to requisition from you the key to the church tower." As he spoke he looked around with his shiny little eyes. "We will take the statues of the riders with us tonight and you can get the key back afterwards at Headquarters. Hurry, we don't have all night," he concluded.

Grandfather reached up slowly for the big iron key that always hung on a peg near the stairs. He handed the key to the soldier. When they had gone, he closed the door and for a moment leaned heavily against it. Johanna saw small drops of perspiration under his nose and on his forehead.

"They will be back as soon as they have seen the riders are gone," Grandmother said. "We will have to hide them better."

"There is no time," Grandfather said. "They will be back in a few minutes, and where can we hide the riders? No, our only chance is somehow to keep them from going upstairs. If we can tell them something that will make them go away, even if it's only for a short time . . ." Grandfather straightened his shoulders and gave Grandmother and Johanna a sly look.

"There is only one thing for us to do. We must try to fool them. We'll act very surprised when we hear the riders are gone and we can even suggest that because they are so old and therefore valuable they must have been stolen."

"They will never believe us," Grandmother said.

"They will certainly be back to investigate, but they might believe us long enough to give us a chance to hide the riders."

Grandmother still looked doubtful, Johanna thought, but Grandfather couldn't talk about it further. The soldiers were back. This time they didn't ring the doorbell. Instead they pounded the stocks of their rifles on the door. The spokesman was hot and red and so angry that he could hardly speak Dutch any more. He kept lapsing into heavy German shouts that Johanna couldn't understand.

"The riders may have been stolen." Grandfather's deep, quiet voice tried to interrupt the angry flow of words. "We all know that they are very valuable."

The big red soldier made so much noise that Johanna didn't think he had heard one word of what Grandfather had said. But now he started to laugh loudly. Sneering, he turned to the other soldiers and mimicked Grandfather. "He thinks they may have been stolen because they are so valuable." And all the soldiers roared with laughter. Suddenly the big soldier turned again towards Grandfather, and he was not laughing now.

"You old liar!" he barked. For a moment Johanna thought that he was going to hit Grandfather. But Grandfather went on talking as if he had not heard him.

"Take me with you to the church tower and I will show you where I left the riders when I last saw them. I never saw them again after I closed the little doors the night the town commander gave us the order to do so."

Grandfather spoke so convincingly that Johanna was almost ready to believe that the riders were now in the possession of some clever thief instead of upstairs in the den under her own bed. But the big soldier didn't care what Grandfather said. He turned his back to him and gave his orders to the other soldiers.

"The old man and the old woman will come with us to Headquarters. The town commander can conduct the hearing himself. If he orders so, we will search the house later. We will not leave a thing unturned, and if those riders are hidden here," he said, shrugging his shoulders in disgust, "we will find them. And these people will learn what happens to those who dare defy an order given by a German officer."

He looked at Johanna. "The child can stay," he said. But he didn't let Johanna kiss Grandfather and Grandmother good-bye. Johanna was standing near the hall cupboard and quickly she slipped down a coat for Grandmother, but she couldn't get Grandfather's coat off the hook. The coat was heavy and the hook too high and now they were leaving. She could give Grandfather only his hat and his woollen scarf, which weren't enough for the chilly September night. Grandfather and Grandmother walked arm in arm out of the door and the soldiers followed them.

When the last soldier slammed the door behind him, Johanna found that her knees were shaking. She had to sit down on the bottom step of the staircase. The clock in the hall ticked and the minutes passed by.

"If those riders are hidden here, these people will learn what happens to those who dare defy an order given by a German officer," the soldier had said.

They must be hidden more safely, Johanna knew, and she would have to do it. The men would certainly not come now. The neighbours must have seen what happened and they would have warned the men to stay far away from the house. Johanna looked out of the peep-hole in the door. One soldier was left standing on guard.

"We will not leave a thing unturned, and if those riders are hidden here, we will find them," the German had also said.

The riders were big and there were twelve of them and the horses, too. What hiding place would be big enough? As she sat on the bottom step of the stairs, Johanna's mind wandered through the whole house, thinking of all the different cupboards, but not one was big enough to hide the riders safely. At last she thought of her attic room. Of course, her own secret hiding place was there. It was certainly big enough, but it was right in Captain Braun's room. But the more she thought about it now, the more she became convinced that it would also be the safest place to hide the riders. The Germans would certainly not think that the riders might be hidden in the room of a German officer and they would probably not search his room. Captain Braun apparently had not discovered the cubbyhole and perhaps never would discover it. Anyhow, it was the only place in the house where she could hide the riders. She would leave them in the burlap sacks and push them all the way deep in.

Tonight was Friday night and Captain Braun was not home. If she worked fast the riders would be hidden before he came back. Johanna ran upstairs and started to carry the sacks to the attic room. She didn't put on a light for fear the soldier on guard would see it and come to investigate; instead, she took Grandfather's torch. She decided to do the heavy work first and carry everything upstairs. Putting the riders in the cubbyhole would be easier. She also decided to take the radio from behind the books and put it in the cubbyhole, too.

It wasn't easy. By the time the last horse and rider were in the attic room Johanna was out of breath. Her hair was mussed up and her skirt was torn in several places. It had also taken her much longer than she had expected, but if she worked fast there was still time enough before Captain Braun came home. In the cupboard she pushed Captain Braun's uniforms aside and reached to open the bolt of the little door, but it had become stiff and rusty. She got down on her knees and tried again. The bolt didn't yield. Johanna felt warm and her hands started to tremble. Surely she would be able to open the bolt, it had never given her trouble before. But no matter how hard she tried, she could not open the bolt on the little door. She forgot everything around her, even the riders and Grandfather and Grandmother and the danger they were in at this moment. She thought only of one thing. The door must open. It must.

She was so busy she didn't hear the footsteps on the stairs or the door of the attic room opening. She first saw Captain Braun when he was standing in the door of the big cupboard. He had to bend down a little, not to hit his head against the low ceiling.

"What are you doing in the dark in my cupboard?" he asked.

He switched the light on so that Johanna's eyes were blinded by it and she turned her head away. Around her on the floor were the sacks with the riders. The radio was right beside her and Johanna pushed it behind her back, but she couldn't hide the riders. Captain Braun kneeled down and opened one of the bags. There was nothing Johanna could do or say. He took out a white horse with gentle black eyes and a fierce curly mane. Then he opened the other bags. The little riders and their horses were lying helpless on their backs on the floor of the cupboard. The legs of the horses were bent as if they wanted to get up and gallop away. The riders looked more brave and proud than ever, but Johanna knew that no matter how brave and proud they looked, they were forever lost and she could not save them any more.

A feeling of reckless despair came over Johanna. Nothing that she would do or say now could make the situation any worse than it was already. She had tried hard but she had failed; she had failed Grandfather and Grandmother and

also the little riders and even her father, whom
she had promised to take care of the little riders.
If it had not been for Captain Braun she could
have saved them. If he hadn't come home early,
the riders would have been hidden and Grandfather and Grandmother would have come back.
Now she didn't know what the Germans might do
to them. Everything she had ever felt against the
Germans welled up suddenly in her.

"I hate you and I despise you," she burst out,
"and so does every decent person, and you'll
never win the war. Grandfather says that you
have already lost it." She talked so fast that she
had to take a deep breath before she could con-
tinue. "And in a few months there will be nothing

left of Germany, Grandmother says. You only have to listen every night to the aeroplanes that fly over."

Then Johanna raised her eyes and looked at Captain Braun for the first time. With his boots and his uniform he looked like all the other Germans. He looked the same as the soldiers who had taken away Grandfather and Grandmother, but his face was different. Captain Braun did not have a soldier's face. He had the face of a flute player. His face was unmoved and, except for a little heightened colour, he appeared not even to have heard what Johanna had said to him.

"So these are the famous little riders," he said quietly. He took one into the room and held it under the light. "They are much more beautiful than I was ever told." He looked again and hesitated for a little while. "I would like to look at them much longer, but it would be safer for them and for you to put them back in the sacks and hide them where they will not be found."

"But I can't," Johanna said. She wasn't feeling angry any more, only very frightened. "The bolt of the door is rusty. I can't open it." She was surprised to hear that she was crying. "And they took Grandfather and Grandmother. They said, 'If we find the riders in this house, you will see what happens to people who disobey an order given by a German officer.' "

Captain Braun kneeled beside Johanna. His hands were strong and quick as he slipped aside the stiff bolt. He took the sacks and started to put the riders back in.

"What will you do to them?" Johanna asked.

"The little riders will be my guests for as long as they want to be," Captain Braun said. "I owe that to them. They are the first Dutchmen who looked at me in a friendly way and did not turn their faces away when I spoke to them."

Johanna felt her face grow hot and red as he spoke. She bent down and started to help him put the riders and the horses back into the sacks.

"There may not be much time," he said. "Crawl through the door and I will hand you the sacks."

Johanna still hesitated. Was he really going to help her?

"Come," he said. "Do as I tell you." There was a faint smile around his mouth, but the rest of his face looked grave. "This is an order given by a German officer." He gave her a gentle push.

In a few minutes the riders were hidden and the radio, too. At a moment when Captain Braun had his back turned, Johanna pushed it deep into the cupboard. One day when he was out she would come and get it. Grandfather couldn't be without his radio.

"Go down now," Captain Braun said. "It's better for all of us if no one sees us together."

Johanna went downstairs and alone she waited in the dark living room. Outside, the soldier was still standing guard. She pushed Grandfather's big chair near the window and sat down, her tired arms leaning on the windowsill. From there she saw them come across the marketplace.

Grandfather had his arm around Grandmother's shoulders as if to protect her from the soldiers who were all around them. This time there were more than nine. As soon as Grandfather opened the door with his key the soldiers swarmed over the room. The big red-faced soldier was again in charge. At his command the others pushed aside the furniture and looked behind it. They stuck their bayonets into the upholstery and ripped it open, although Johanna couldn't understand why. The riders and the horses were much too big to be hidden in the upholstery of a chair. With their rifles they knocked on the walls, and when Grandmother's Delft-blue plates tumbled from the wall and broke into pieces some of the soldiers laughed. When they left to search the upstairs, the room looked as if a tornado had passed through.

Grandfather and Grandmother went upstairs, too, but they were always surrounded by soldiers so that Johanna could not speak one word to them. All she could do was follow. The big red-faced soldier told Grandfather to turn on the light, and while he fumbled clumsily to find the switch, the soldier pushed Grandfather aside and turned the switch himself. In the soft glow of the lamp the den looked immaculate. Johanna could hear Grandmother give a little gasp of surprise.

The soldiers began with the desk, taking out the drawers and dumping the contents in a heap on the floor. They went through all the papers. Now and then one of the soldiers went over to the red-faced man to let him read something. He always shook his head and shrugged his shoulders.

At last they went to the bookcase and began to take out the books. Johanna saw Grandfather's face grow tight. She wished she could show him somehow that there was nothing to worry about, but there was always at least one soldier standing next to him and Grandmother. The soldiers reached the shelf where the radio was always hidden, but there were only the books they kept dumping on the floor. Now they went down on their knees and looked under the bed and knocked on the wooden floor. Over their bent heads Grandfather looked at Johanna with more pride than she had ever before seen in his eyes. Grandmother gave Johanna a little wink.

The soldiers finally gave up. They realised that there was nothing hidden in these rooms. Only the attic room was left. They climbed the last stairs. Johanna felt weak and shaky again. Even when they found Captain Braun, they might still decide to search the room. She was glad now that Grandfather and Grandmother had no idea where the riders were hidden. They walked confidently up the stairs, Grandmother winking again at Johanna behind the soldiers' backs.

The soldiers could not have been informed that this room was occupied by one of their own officers, because they were taken aback when they found Captain Braun with his legs on the table, writing in his music book. He rose from his chair. The soldiers apologised profusely and the red-faced man especially seemed extremely upset at having intruded so unceremoniously into the room of a German officer. Captain Braun put all of them at ease with a few friendly words, and he must have made a joke, for they laughed. For one terrible moment Johanna thought that, after all, Captain Braun's face looked no different from all the other soldiers. What he had done tonight could be a trap and he could betray them. But the soldiers now made ready to go, and they went without searching the room. Captain Braun swung his legs back onto the table and took up his pencil and music book.

The attitude of the soldiers changed during their walk downstairs. When they came they had been sure they would find the riders. Now they seemed uncertain. The big red-faced soldier seemed to take it very much to heart that he had failed to find the riders or even to find any evidence that Grandfather had anything to do with their disappearance. He and the other soldiers seemed suddenly to be in a terrible hurry and they left the house without saying a word, except for one young man with a pale complexion and fair hair whom Johanna had hardly noticed before. He stopped on the doorstep to talk to Grandfather.

"We hope you understand, sir, that we only did our duty. Our duty is more important than the little inconvenience we caused you." His pale face started to glow now with enthusiasm and he raised his right hand. "Heil Hitler," he shouted as

Grandfather closed the door behind him.

Grandfather picked up Johanna and swung her high in the air, as he had done when she was still a little girl.

"Oh, Johanna, we are so proud of you, but where in this house did you hide the little riders?"

Grandmother hugged Johanna, but she wouldn't let her tell the secret until they were all sitting quietly with a warm drink. "We will clean up the rooms tomorrow," Grandmother said and she didn't even look at her Delft-blue plates. She could look only at Johanna. They talked till deep into the night and both Grandfather and Grandmother went upstairs with Johanna to tuck her in and kiss her good night.

"Will they ever come back?" Johanna asked Grandfather.

"I don't think so," he said as he sat down on the edge of her bed. "They are convinced that the riders are not hidden here and they can't prove that I ever had anything to do with their disappearance." He turned off the light and left the room.

As Johanna lay thinking about everything that had happened during the long day, she could hear the aeroplanes flying over the house. The night was almost gone and, with the daylight, the planes were returning from their mission. Every night it sounded as if there were more planes than the night before. This time Johanna didn't think of her father; instead she thought of Captain Braun. She put on her slippers and walked upstairs. The door of the room stood ajar. Johanna pushed it open. Captain Braun was sitting at the table with his face buried in his hands. He looked up when he heard Johanna.

"I cannot sleep," Johanna said. "If I leave my door open, would you please play the flute for me?"

Chapter Five

The winter started early that year. In November the weather was already bitter cold with sleet and snow and an icy wind that blew from the northeast over the flatlands below the sea. The fuel rations were far too small to heat the whole house. Grandfather and Grandmother closed off the downstairs of the house and moved upstairs to the den. With the pot-bellied stove blazing red, the den sometimes looked almost cosy, Johanna thought. But even the little stove used up too much of the fuel that had to last all through the winter. Sometimes Dirk came and brought them a little load of wood, but often Grandfather and Johanna went out with the axe and saw to chop down a small tree in the park at the edge of the town.

Each time Johanna remembered how she had walked there with Grandfather on summer evenings in the early years of the war. The park had always been shady and cool with the big old linden trees, and the whole town had smelled of their blossoms. Along the stream that flowed through the park stood the willow trees from which Grandfather used to cut whistles for Johanna. Now the old trees had all been chopped down by the Germans for fuel, leaving the park bare and mutilated with only dark stumps sticking out from the stiff and frozen earth. The soldiers had left so few trees that Grandfather and Johanna had to go far down the stream to find even a small young willow tree. Grandfather was handy with an axe and saw and, after Johanna had piled the wood neatly on her sledge, together they pulled their precious load home, pausing from time to time to blow life back into their frozen hands.

Almost worse than the cold and the shortage of fuel was the hunger. Johanna had never felt really hungry before, but now she often woke in the middle of the night with a tight, empty feeling in her stomach, almost like a pain. Sometimes Grandmother would put an apple, if she had one, on the table next to Johanna's bed and Johanna would eat it very slowly. After that it was easier to fall asleep. But as the winter went on, it became harder and harder to get apples or any other food. On days when it wasn't too cold, Grandfather and Johanna went foraging in the country on their bicycles. Their bicycles now had wooden tires and they were so heavy to push against the strong, cold wind that Grandfather and Johanna never got far. Usually they ended up at Dirk's farm. Dirk never sent anybody away with empty hands and so they came home with milk and a small bag of wheat and sometimes even a few eggs.

Captain Braun wasn't home much during these winter months. His attic room was so cold that he spent most of the days at the barracks, returning late at night when everybody was already asleep and leaving again early in the morning when nobody was up yet.

On a day when Captain Braun was away from his room as usual, Johanna slipped up to the attic to get the radio for Grandfather. The bolt on the door of the cubbyhole moved easily now and she knew exactly where she had put the radio. She didn't dare take out the little riders and look at them, but they seemed safe and snug in their warm sacks. Through a sack she could feel the sturdy legs of one of the galloping horses. She smiled and closed the door.

The attic was very cold and the room had a lost and lonesome look. Captain Braun's flute was, as always, lying on the table. He seldom played now. Johanna wondered if it was because of the aeroplanes going over or because his hands were too stiff from the cold. Sometimes at night she lay awake, hoping to hear music again, and sometimes if she got up and made a great deal of noise about opening her door, after a time the thin pure voice of the flute would come floating down from the attic.

Grandfather and Grandmother never spoke to Captain Braun about the night he helped Johanna hide the riders. At first they had waited for Captain Braun to mention it to them, but he had never said a word except for a polite "Good morning" or "Good evening".

"It is probably better for us not to interfere," Grandfather said. "That was something between Captain Braun and Johanna and we had better leave it that way. It must not have been easy for him to hide the riders from his own people."

But Grandfather never looked at Captain Braun in the cold forbidding way he had before and Grandmother sometimes even spoke a few words with him about the weather.

Not only did the winter start early that year, it lasted endlessly long. In April Grandfather and Johanna still had to go out and get wood, hoping every time that this would be the last load they would need. The food rations were down to almost nothing and the only things that kept the people alive were the hopeful news bulletins. The war couldn't last much longer. Soon Germany would surrender.

The day Germany surrendered was a beautiful warm day in May, just as it had been five years ago when the German troops entered Holland. Grandfather came home and stretched his arms out towards Grandmother.

"It is all over. We are free again."

He kissed Grandmother and for one moment Johanna didn't realise why they looked so different. Then she saw what she had never seen before: their eyes were full of tears.

She left them together and went upstairs to the den. From behind the books she took the radio and put it on the table. She turned it on loud. There was nothing to be afraid of any more. She turned on the Dutch station and then a few others and every one told the same news. Germany had surrendered unconditionally.

They will never march any more and sing their horrible songs while they go through our town, she thought. And I will never have to be afraid any more that their footsteps will stop at our door. After that happened once I have always waited for it to happen again, but now it never will.

She went downstairs and found Grandfather and Grandmother in the living room. Grandmother was looking proudly at Grandfather, who had just changed his clothes and was wearing, for the first time openly, the uniform of the Dutch underground army – a simple navy-blue overall with a holster and gun. All through the winter he had looked old and thin, but now he looked young again and strong and triumphant.

"Come," Grandfather said. "We'll take our first walk in our free town."

The streets were full of people. Here and there small troops of soldiers were starting their retreat, heavily packed, riding old, rickety bicycles. Even though it had been so long ago and Johanna had been a very young girl, she still remembered when the German troops had entered the town. How arrogantly they had paraded through the streets of the town that they rode through now so silently and quickly, hoping nobody would notice them.

In the afternoon Captain Braun knocked on the door of the den as they were just starting their lunch. Next to him stood the same heavy sack that he had brought with him almost a year ago. He seemed ready to leave.

"I came to say good-bye," he said to Grandfather and Grandmother, making one of his stiff little bows and smiling at Johanna. "We've had our orders to retreat as fast as we can from here, but I could not go without saying good-bye to you."

Grandfather and Grandmother got up from their chairs. Grandmother was the first to reach out her hand to him.

"I hope," she said, "you will find everybody well when you get home."

"Oh yes." Captain Braun's face lit up. "Thank God, my parents and my wife and our little boy are safe." He kissed Grandmother's hand. "I am not sorry to leave," he continued. "I hated the war and I'm glad it's all over, but I shall miss the little riders. I have often taken them out from their hiding place during my lonesome evenings and I wished I could have seen them ride on their white horses."

He stretched his hand hesitantly towards Grandfather. "I wish you and them the best of everything."

"Maybe," Grandfather said slowly, "maybe many, many years from now, when this terrible war is not so fresh in our memory, when we have been able to forget a little, you will come back and see them ride in their full glory over our town."

Captain Braun looked Grandfather straight in the eyes. "Is that an invitation?" he asked.

Grandfather hesitated. "I think so," he finally said, and he shook Captain Braun's hand.

Captain Braun bent down and kissed Johanna's hand, just as he had done with Grandmother.

"There is something," he said to Johanna,

"that I didn't want to take with me. Our trip will probably be rough and hard and I didn't want any harm to come to it. I left it for you upstairs."

He clicked his heels and bowed again and reached for his sack. Grandfather offered to help carry it down, but Captain Braun laughed as he refused and swung the heavy sack over his shoulder. He walked quickly downstairs without looking back. Johanna heard the front door close behind him. Captain Braun was gone.

Although they had just started lunch, nobody was hungry any more. Johanna waited till Grandfather and Grandmother had gone downstairs; then she started up to her attic room. Halfway up the creaking stairs she sat down, trying to picture how everything would be now that the Germans had gone.

Tonight, she thought, I'll sleep again in my room. Soon the riders will be back and I will hear the carillon play again when I am just about to fall asleep. But I won't hear the flute. I never will hear it again.

She walked slowly up the rest of the stairs. Carefully she opened the door. The room was light as the sun streamed in through the open window, making a pattern of stripes on the floor and on the walls. The wood of the table shone with sunlight, as if it had just been polished. Johanna's eyes had to get used to the bright light after the dark stairway. Then she saw the velvet case with the embroidered mountain flowers lying on the table. In it was the flute. A note lay next to it. Johanna went over and sat down on the windowsill. The sunlight seemed sharp and her eyes started to sting as she read the words slowly.

To a brave girl, from her friend – Wilhelm Braun.

The next day the Allied soldiers arrived in town. They were Canadians. The streets were so packed with cheering people that the men in blue overalls had difficulty keeping order. At first a single man on a motorbike came. He raced with terrific speed through the town and was gone before the people realised that they had seen the first Canadian. For a few hours nothing happened. Then the jeeps came and trucks loaded with soldiers. They didn't look at all like soldiers, Johanna thought. They looked tremendously healthy with beautifully clean, crisp uniforms. They smiled and waved their caps. Nobody could ever be afraid of these soldiers, Johanna decided. They tried to talk to her, but she couldn't understand the strange words. The soldiers laughed and stuffed her pockets with wonderful things that Johanna hadn't seen in years. Chocolates and other sweets, delightful-smelling soap that she would give Grandmother and cigarettes for Grandfather.

The people were wild with joy and relief, and there was nothing but feasting these first wonderful days of freedom. Then the town began to prepare for the official celebration of its liberation. Grandfather and Johanna went to work to make the little riders ready so that they could return to the church steeple in time for the celebration. During the day Grandfather was busy in town, but in the evenings after supper he and Johanna went to the church tower together. Grandfather worked on the mechanism while Johanna cleaned and polished the riders and the horses, who had become a little dusty in their hiding place. They always worked till dark.

One evening when Grandfather was working late, Johanna went over to the oval window in the church tower and looked out over the marketplace. Small groups of soldiers were leisurely strolling around. They stopped in the middle of the marketplace and pointed at the old church and some of the old houses. Then from the other side of the marketplace came a tall soldier. He didn't walk leisurely as the other soldiers did, nor did he walk as if he were a soldier in a strange city. He walked deliberately, as if he had a purpose and as if he knew his way.

It's just as if this happened once before, Johanna thought. As if I saw him once long ago coming towards me while I was standing at the window.

The soldier walked so fast that Johanna, who could see only the opposite side of the marketplace, lost sight of him. Still, she thought of him as she watched the scene below, more soldiers and some children playing ball. Now a soldier caught the ball and threw it back to the laughing children.

Grandfather was ready to go now, and it was almost dark in the church tower. Johanna helped Grandfather pack his tools in the tool-box. They would have to work only a few more nights and the little riders would be ready to ride again on their horses. Johanna was just saying good night to them when the hinges of the door of the church tower squeaked.

"That's Grandmother, Johanna," Grandfather said, "to see what we are doing here together in the dark."

"We are coming," Johanna shouted, as she rushed towards the staircase.

But at the bottom of the stairs she didn't see
Grandmother. Instead she saw the tall soldier
whom she had watched coming across the marketplace. He took off his cap as he looked up to
Johanna and Grandfather standing at the top of
the stairs.

Grandfather stood still for one second, looking
down at the soldier. Then, without saying a word,
he started to run down the stairs.

I always knew he would come to take me back
home with him, Johanna thought as she started to

run after Grandfather. And because she wasn't carrying a heavy tool-box she could run faster than Grandfather. Halfway down the stairs she overtook him and pushed him aside. She ran down the last few stairs and straight into her father's outstretched arms. But how strange that I ever thought I had forgotten what he looked like, she thought. I would have recognised him anywhere.

Chapter Six

Johanna was sitting on the windowsill in her attic room, her window opened wide, waiting for the clock on the church steeple to strike twelve. Today was the day the town would officially celebrate its liberation. Down below lay the marketplace. Many people were already gathered and still more came streaming from the narrow sidestreets. From all the old houses flags were flying, bright with colour, red, white and blue. They seemed to romp with the strong warm wind, as if they wanted to make up for the five years they had been lying hidden in dusty attics or cupboards. Behind the doors underneath the church steeple, the little riders were waiting, their hands clasping the swords, ready to salute each other.

Grandfather and Grandmother and Johanna's father were down in the marketplace, but Johanna wanted to watch the little riders from her own room, where she had always watched them and where she could see them best. She let her eyes wander over the marketplace. Grandfather and Grandmother were standing close together and next to them stood Dirk. He waved his cap at Johanna when Grandfather pointed her out to him. Then all Grandfather's friends waved to her.

The mayor climbed onto a rostrum and started to speak. Johanna leaned as far out of the window as she could, but she couldn't hear the words he spoke. Besides, she was looking for her father, whom she saw now squeezing through the crowd of people and motioning with his hands to Johanna that he was coming up to her.

"I also decided to watch from here," he said when he finally got upstairs. "This is the best place in the whole town to watch the little riders." He sat next to her on the windowsill. While outside the mayor was talking, Johanna's father took her hand. "We have had so little time to talk together," he said. "There has never been a quiet moment for just the two of us. But now I'll tell you the plans Mother and I made."

Father told her that soon, when his military

service was over, he was going to buy a farm and they would all become farmers.

"I have always loved the sea," Father said, "and I still do, but it takes me away from home too much and already we have lost five whole years. From now on we'll always be together and we'll often come to Holland to visit Grandfather and Grandmother and to see the little riders. I promise you that."

"Do you think I can learn to play the flute in America?" Johanna asked. She got up from her seat and showed Captain Braun's flute to Father.

"Of course you can, my little Johanna," Father said. "And I know you will learn to play the flute beautifully."

Johanna shook her head. "Not as beautifully as Captain Braun," she said. "He was a German but I couldn't really hate him even when I tried, after I heard him play the flute. And then he helped us, and sometimes I wish I could hear him play the flute again."

Father gave the flute back to Johanna and she held it in her hand. Together they looked down upon the many people. It was almost twelve o'clock now and the mayor had stopped speaking.

A deep silence fell over the marketplace. From the top of the church steeple the flag was flying at half-mast. In the three minutes before the clock struck twelve, the town thought of all the people who had died during the five years of occupation – the young men and women who had fought for the freedom of their country and who would never return, and the old people and children who had died from starvation during the last winter of the war. Then the clock started to strike the hour and the flag was hoisted to the top.

Behind her eyes Johanna felt a sharp prickly feeling as she watched the little doors. In one hand she still held the flute; with the other she squeezed her father's hand very tightly. In the marketplace everybody looked up at the church steeple as the clock struck the last note.

"Here they come," Father said to Johanna.

And while the carillon started to play its tunes into the blue summer sky, the two little doors underneath the church steeple opened and out rode the little riders. They rode out, proud and beautiful as ever, over a free town and its jubilant people.

KICK-OFF
Hannah Cole

Paula and Shazia know that they're just as good at football as most of the boys – the problem is getting the chance to prove it. But when Mr Crendon, the P.E. teacher, picks the school team, the two girls are determined to be in it.

"Hannah Cole has looked clearly at her audience, aimed her book squarely at them, and scored... A well-paced story."
School Librarian

"Smartly up to date in its case for unisex soccer."
Chris Powling, The Times Educational Supplement

"Highly readable."
The Scotsman

THE RUSSIAN DOLL
Joan Smith

Moscow doesn't seem a very welcoming place to Miranda, although being with bossy Great Aunt Lotty is hardly a help in making friends. For G.A. always speaks her mind very loudly and usually manages to upset somebody. Fortunately, however, like the doll G.A. insists on buying Miranda, there's a lot more to Mother Russia than at first appears!

A lively story for young readers, *The Russian Doll* offers a fascinating glimpse of everyday life in the fast-changing Russia of today.

"Up-to-date... Convincing atmosphere."
Susan Hill, The Sunday Times

EARTHQUAKE
Ruskin Bond

"What do you do when there's an earthquake?" asks Rakesh. Everyone in the Burman household has their own ideas, but when the tremors begin and everything starts to shake and quake, to crack and crumble, they are all taken by surprise...

"The stories are original and well written, the presentation examplary... Lovely stuff."
The Junior Bookshelf

MORE WALKER PAPERBACKS

For You to Enjoy